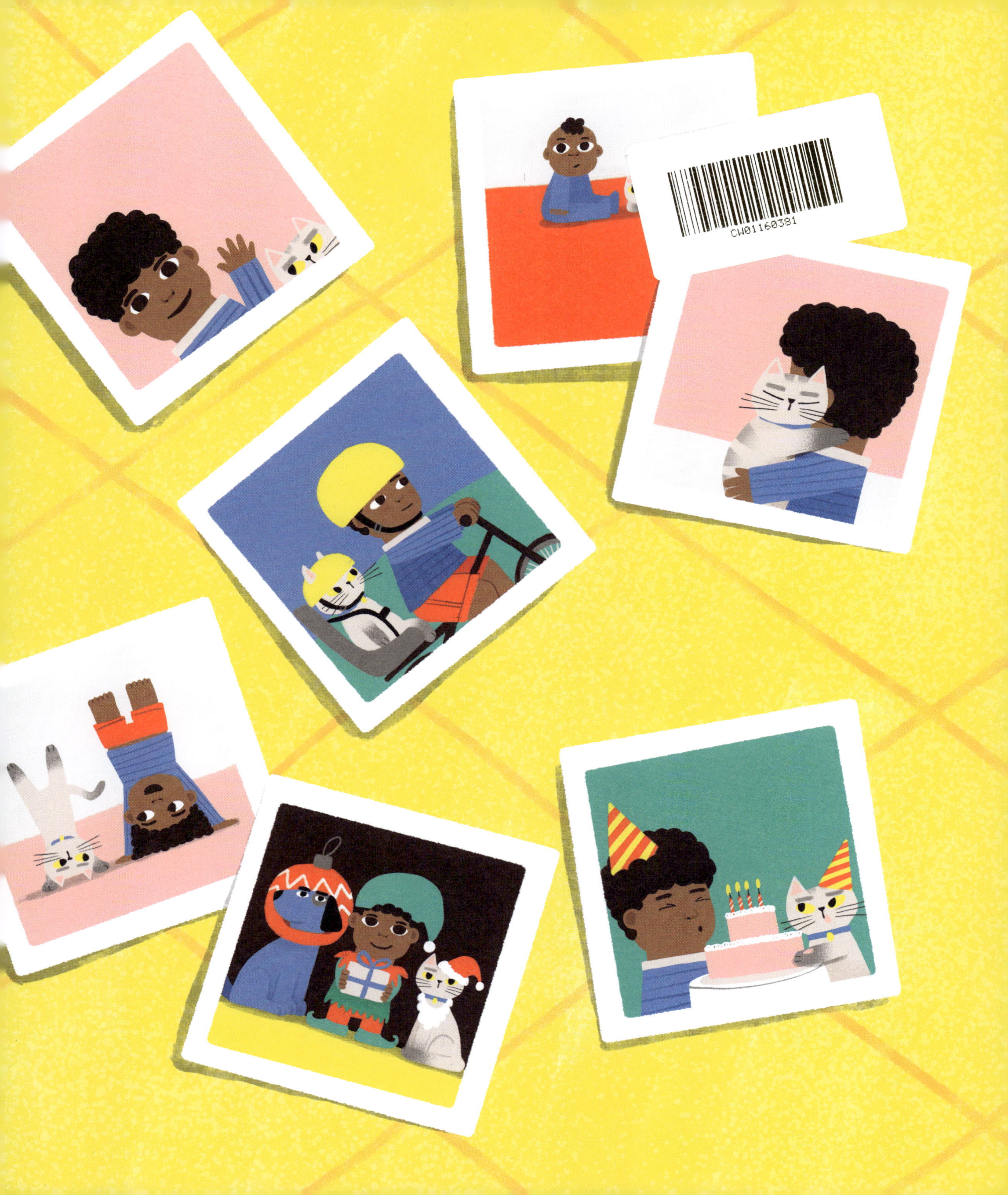

For Tove and Elliot.
Thank you for all the inspiration.

First edition published in 2025 by Flying Eye Books,
27 Westgate Street, London, E8 3RL.
www.flyingeyebooks.com

Represented by: Authorised Rep Compliance Ltd.
Ground Floor, 71 Lower Baggot Street, Dublin, D02 P593, Ireland.
www.arccompliance.com

Text and illustrations © Donna Smith Fredin 2025.
Donna Smith Fredin has asserted her right under the Copyright, Designs and Patents Act, 1988, to be identified as the Author and Illustrator of this Work.

All rights reserved. No part of this publication may be reproduced or transmitted in any form or by any means, electronic or mechanical, including photocopying, recording or by any information and storage retrieval system, without prior written consent from the publisher.

1 3 5 7 9 10 8 6 4 2

Edited by Fay Evans
Designed by Lilly Gottwald

UK ISBN: 978-1-83874-331-4
US ISBN: 978-1-83874-290-4

Published in the US by Flying Eye Books Ltd
Printed in Poland on FSC® certified paper.

FSC
www.fsc.org
MIX
Paper | Supporting responsible forestry
FSC® C163799

Donna Fredin

THAT'S NOT STELLA

Flying Eye Books

Milo and Stella are best friends.
They do everything together.

But for the past few days, something has felt a little different . . .

Milo is not sure that this is Stella.

Yesterday afternoon, Milo found Stella sleeping in the green cat bed.

Milo knows that Stella does not like the green cat bed. It is itchy and smells like old cheese. Her favourite place to sleep is the big blue armchair.

"That's not Stella,"

Milo said to his mum.

"Of course it is," said Milo's Mum.
"Maybe she is trying something different today."

In the morning, Milo saw Stella walking on the top of the tall fence.

Milo knows that Stella is scared of heights. She once got stuck in a big tree and had to be rescued.

"That's NOT Stella,"

Milo said to his mum.

"Of course it is," said Milo's Mum. "She's just being adventurous today."

That afternoon, Milo saw Stella eating the dry cat food. Milo knows that Stella does not like dry cat food. She hides it under the stairs.

"THAT'S NOT STELLA!"

Milo said, loudly.

"Of course it is," said Milo's Mum. "Who else would it be?"

Milo took a deep breath . . .

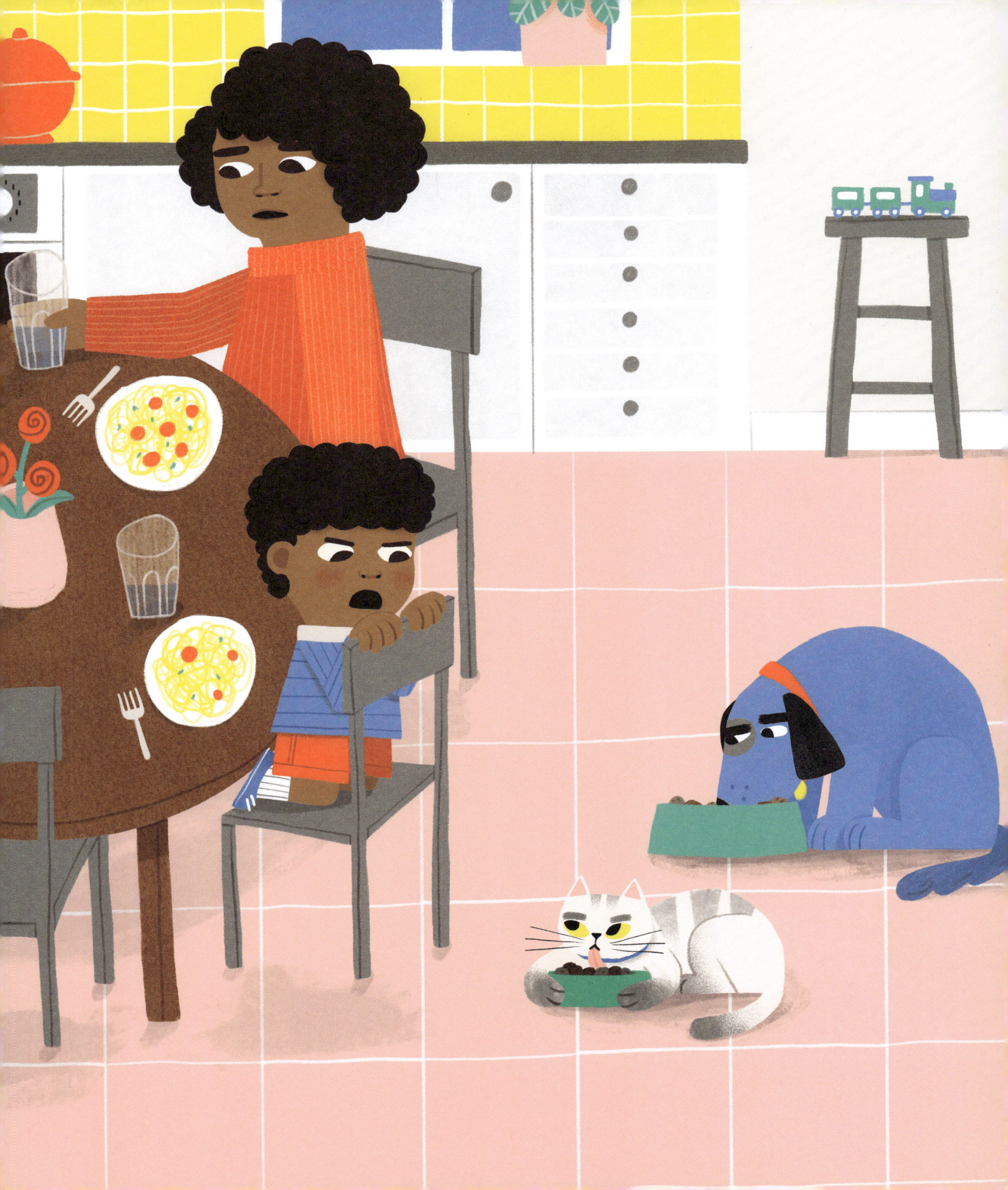

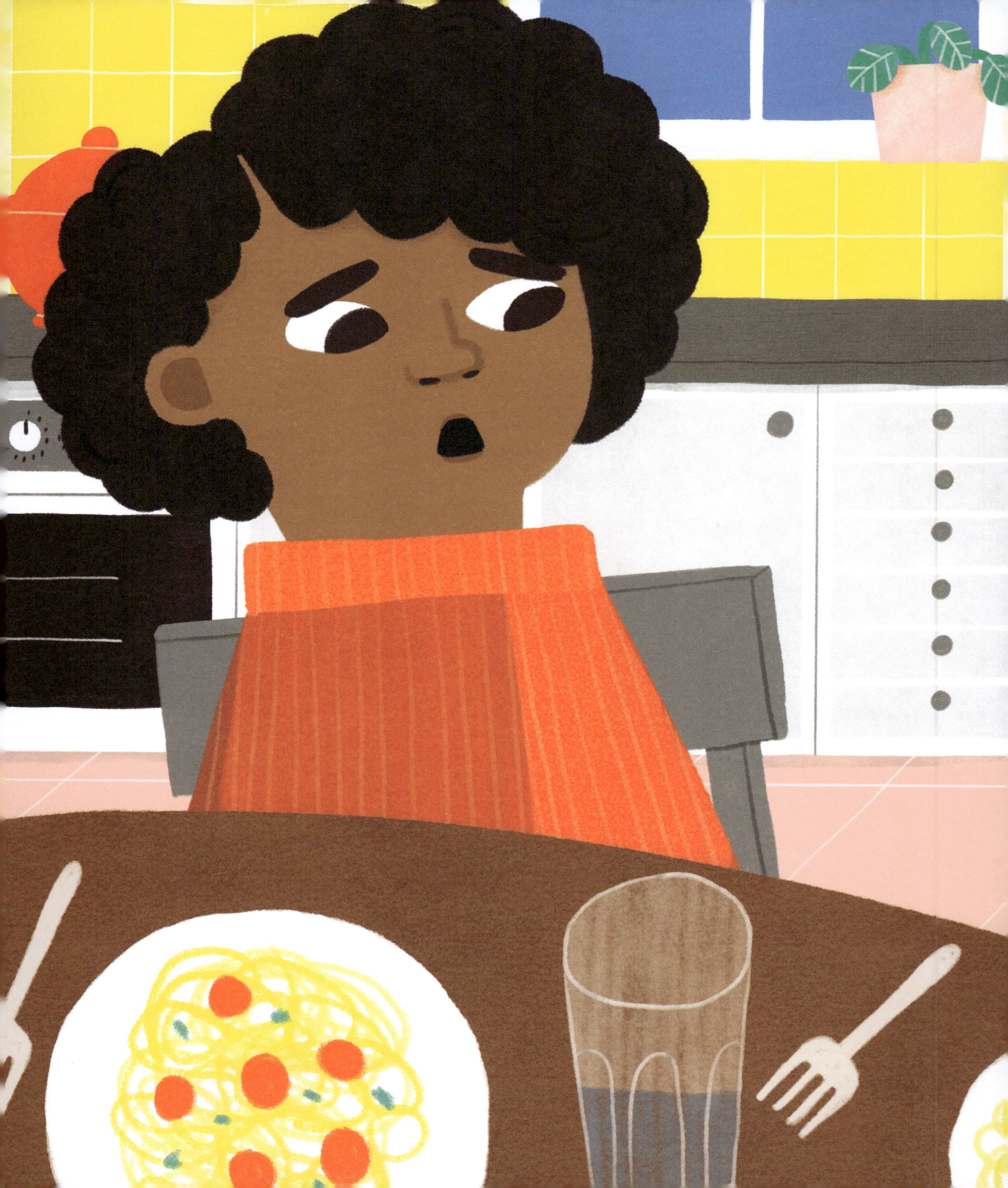

"I DON'T KNOW, BUT IT'S NOT STELLA!"

Milo's Mum decided to check the cats collar. She read out the letters. "S-T-E-L-L-A. You see, Milo?" She said. "It is definitely her."

Milo was surprised. It really didn't feel like Stella, but he couldn't prove it. Maybe he was wrong after all . . .

That night, while everyone else was sleeping, there was a meeting in the garden.

shhhh

The two cats looked at each other. They were almost identical, apart from the fact that the left cat was ever so slightly darker than the right cat.

The cat on the right removed the collar from its neck and passed it to the cat on the left. "Meow," it said and then headed off into the night.

The next morning, Milo decided to find Stella to give her a big hug. He missed playing with his best friend.

He looked down at her, sleeping peacefully in her favourite chair . . .

. . . and noticed a suitcase sticking out from behind the couch. It had fallen open, so he took a look inside.

Milo could not believe his eyes. Inside the suitcase were sea shells, postcards and a lot of photos of a cat that looked remarkably like Stella.

PAWFECT MATCH
The Pet Lookalike Agency

Milo grabbed the suitcase and rushed off to show his Mum.

Milo began showing his mum the contents of the suitcase. He handed her the photos, plane tickets, receipts for cat food . . .

"Its funny," Milo said, looking at one of the photos. "That dog looks just like Rufus..."

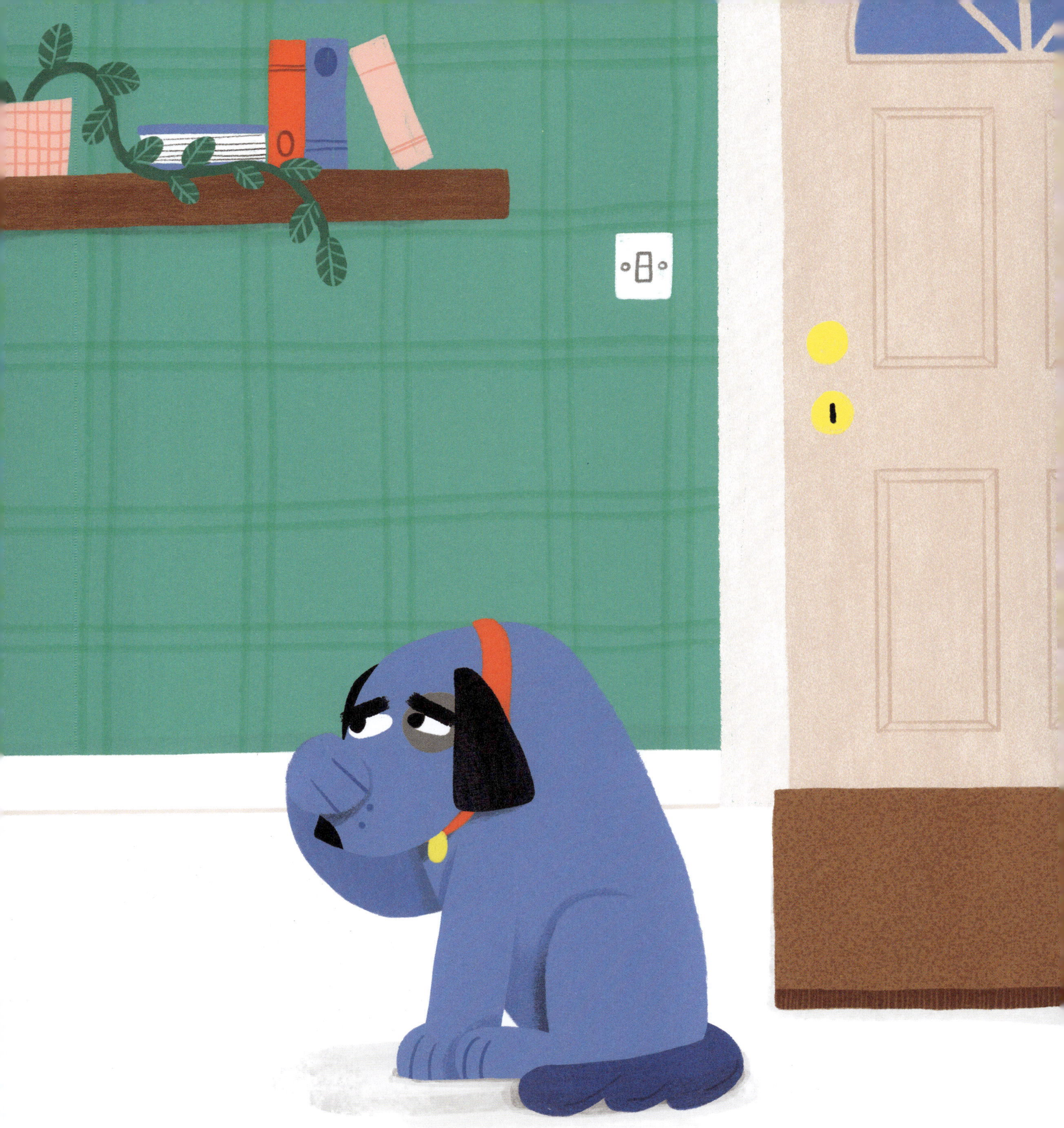

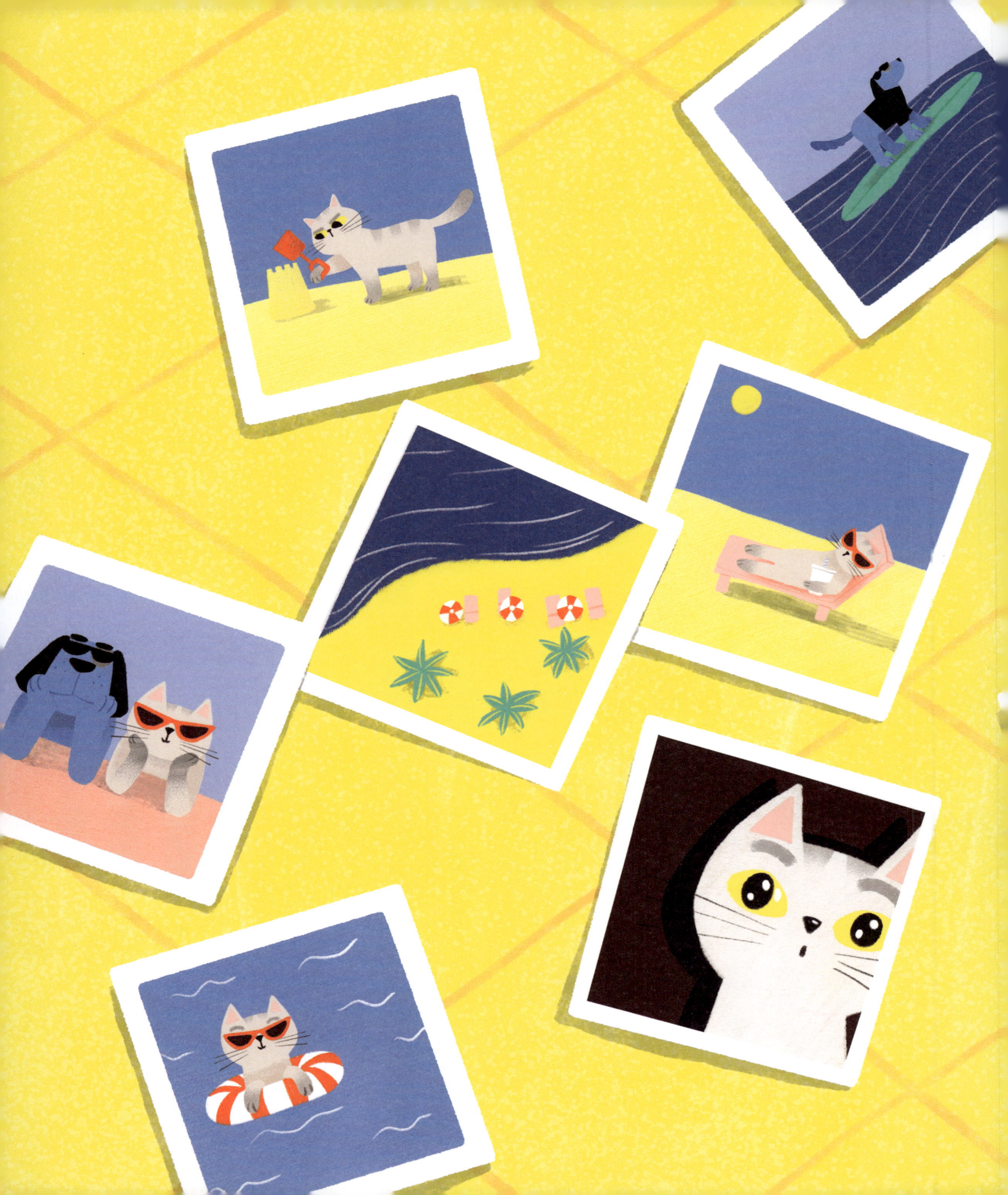